Aaaarrgghh, Spider!

Lydia Monks

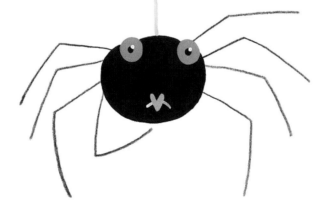

EGMONT

It's really lonely being a spider. I want to be a family pet.

THIS family's pet!

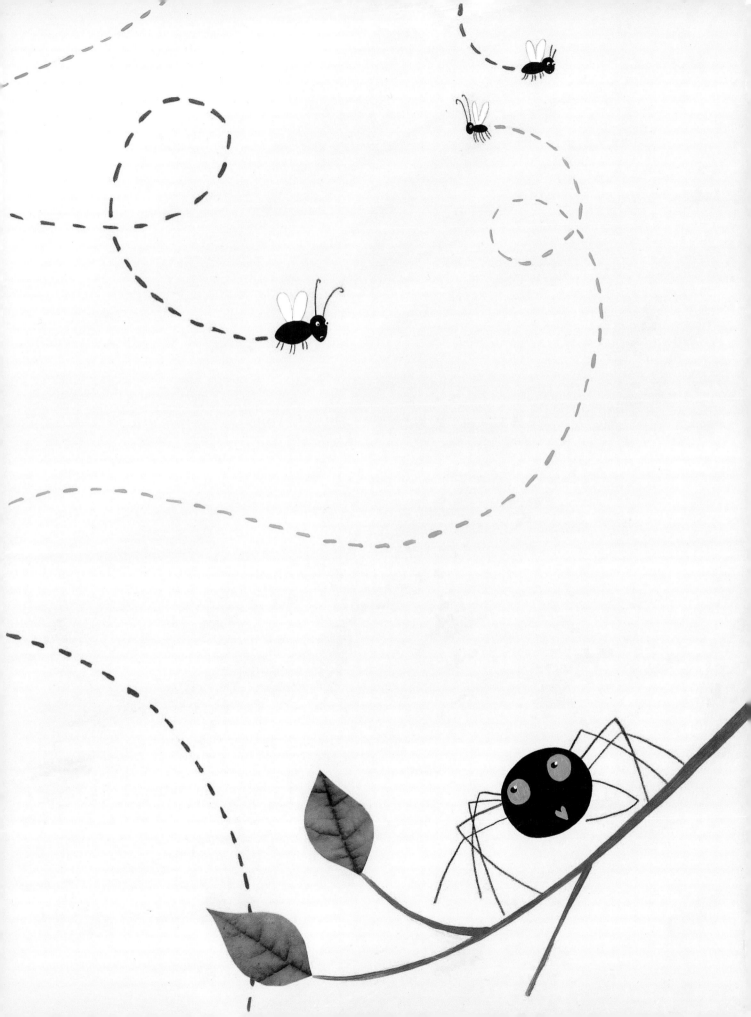

First published in Great Britain in 2004 by Egmont Books Limited, 239 Kensington High Street, London W8 6SA.

Text and illustrations copyright © Lydia Monks 2004.

Lydia Monks has asserted her moral rights.

ISBN 1 4052 1044 3 (paperback) ISBN 1 4052 0688 8 (hardback)

A CIP catalogue record for this title is available from The British Library.

Printed in Singapore   10 9 8 7

for Marcus

I know!
I'll show them what a great dancer I am.
None of their pets can dance like me!

"Look at me! Watch me dance!"

"Out

you

go!"

Oh dear!

I know!
I'll show them
how clean
I am.

None of their
pets are clean
like me!

"Out

you

go!"

Oh dear!

I know!
I'll show them how easy
I am to look after.

None of their
pets can feed
themselves
like I can!

"Out

you

go!"

It's no good.
This family will
never want me.

I'm going to go
and live all alone . . .

. . . . in the garden.

"Look out here, everybody!"

I'm a real, true, proper pet!

In fact, I'm so happy with my new family,
I think I'll introduce them to all my friends . . .